W9-ABU-768

DISNEY'S THE LITTLE MERMAID

ADVANCE PUBLISHERS

Published by Advance Publishers, L.C.
Maitland, FL 32751 USA
www.advancepublishers.com
Produced by Judy O Productions, Inc.
Designed by SunDried Penguin
© 2006 Disney Enterprises, Inc.
The Little Mermaid
Printed in the United States of America

Once upon a time, there was a little mermaid named Ariel who dreamed of living in the human world. She loved to go on adventures with her best friend, Flounder, and on the day of the royal concert, instead of performing with her sisters, she explored a shipwreck and swam up to the surface to look around.

When Ariel remembered about the royal concert, she rushed home. The evil octopus sea witch, Ursula, watched her go, hoping to find a way to cause trouble for King Triton, Ariel's father. The King was very angry that Ariel had swam up to the surface. He ordered her never to go there again and asked Sebastian the crab to keep an eye on her.

Sebastian followed Ariel and Flounder to an underwater cave where Ariel had a collection of treasures from the human world. Ariel saw a ship overhead and went to watch the humans on board, especially a handsome young man, Prince Eric. Suddenly, there was a terrible storm and as the Prince tried to save his crew, an explosion sent him overboard. Ariel was horrified and swam to his rescue.

Ariel carried Prince Eric to the beach and fell instantly in love with him. She started to sing to him but as he awoke, Ariel disappeared into the sea. Prince Eric knew he would never forget the voice of the beautiful girl who had rescued him. Meanwhile, Ursula had watched the rescue and knew that Ariel's love for Prince Eric was the way to destroy King Triton's kingdom.

Back at the underwater palace, King Triton discovered Ariel had rescued a human and fallen in love with him. He was so angry that he destroyed all her treasures. Ariel was very upset and when Ursula's evil eels, Flotsam and Jetsam, showed up and suggested they take her to Ursula for help, she agreed.

Ursula told Ariel that she could turn her into a human – but at a price. "You must give me your voice," she said. In return, Ariel would be human for three days, but if the Prince hadn't given her a kiss of true love by sunset on the third day she would turn back into a mermaid and, "You will belong to me!" cried the sea witch. Ariel agreed and signed Ursula's contract – then she was turned into a human and swam to the beach.

When Prince Eric found Ariel, he didn't know who she was and Ariel couldn't tell him as she no longer had a voice. He took Ariel to his palace and showed her his kingdom. By the second day, he had begun to fall in love with her and took her for a romantic boat ride on the lagoon. But just as they were about to kiss, Flotsam and Jetsam appeared and overturned the boat.

That night, Ursula decided to take matters into her own tentacles and changed herself into a beautiful young girl named Vanessa. She put Ariel's voice in a shell around her neck and made her way to the palace. When Prince Eric heard the lovely voice coming from the shell, he recognized it as belonging to the girl who saved his life and agreed to marry Vanessa the next day.

When Ariel awoke to the news of Prince Eric and Vanessa's wedding aboard a special royal wedding ship, she was heartbroken. But then Ariel's sea friends discovered that Vanessa was really Ursula and raced to tell Ariel. Together, they set out to the wedding ship to stop the marriage.

As Ariel climbed on board, her seagull friends managed to shatter Vanessa's necklace – revealing her as the evil Ursula and setting Ariel's voice free. Prince Eric realized who Ariel really was – but it was too late! The sun was setting and Ariel had turned back into a mermaid. Ursula dragged Ariel into the sea with her.

But King Triton was waiting for them. Ursula agreed to set Ariel free if King Triton took her place as Ursula's prisoner. The King gave Ursula his crown and magic trident and signed a new contract. But just then Prince Eric appeared and fought Ursula, finally destroying her by driving his ship through her cold heart. At last, the ocean was free from Ursula's evil rule!

King Triton could see how unhappy Ariel was without her true love, so he used his magic trident to turn Ariel back into a human! Ariel's wish had come true and she and Prince Eric lived happily ever after.

The End